PUFFIN BOOKS

ADVENTURES OF ZOT THE DOG

Zot the Dog and his best friend Clive have all sorts
of funny adventures and come across lots of
curious characters, including Mrs Mouse, Addy
Snake, Frog and Fowly Fox, who disguises him-
self as Old Duck!

Ivan Jones has been a teacher and Education
Officer and is now a full-time writer. He con-
tributes to various magazines, including *The Times
Educational Supplement*, and is a regular
broadcaster on Radio Shropshire. He lives in
Shropshire and has three children.

Ivan Jones

Adventures of Zot the Dog

Illustrated by
Judy Brown

PUFFIN BOOKS

For Lara, Levin and Jessica

PUFFIN BOOKS

Published by the Penguin Group
27 Wrights Lane, London W8 5TZ, England
Viking Penguin Inc., 40 West 23rd Street, New York, New York 10010, USA
Penguin Books Australia Ltd, Ringwood, Victoria, Australia
Penguin Books Canada Ltd, 2801 John Street, Markham, Ontario, Canada L3R 1B4
Penguin Books (NZ) Ltd, 182–190 Wairau Road, Auckland 10, New Zealand

Penguin Books Ltd, Registered Offices: Harmondsworth, Middlesex, England

Zot and Mrs Mouse first published by Gemini Book 1982
This collection first published by Viking Kestrel 1987
Published in Puffin Books 1989
10 9 8 7 6 5 4 3 2 1

Copyright © Ivan Jones, 1982, 1987
Illustrations copyright © Judy Brown, 1987
All rights reserved

Made and printed in Great Britain by
Richard Clay Ltd, Bungay, Suffolk
Filmset in Linotron Times

Contents

Zot and
Mrs Mouse

In a little old house, down a
little old lane, nearly hidden by
trees and the humps of old pit
mounds, live Zot the dog and
his best friend, Clive.

"Let's search for mice, today," Zot said to Clive as they went out. So they peeped into woody cracks and pried into broken boxes and peered into dingy holes.

"There's one!" woofed Zot.
They chased the mouse. The
mouse dived into a hole by the
root of a tree. Clive dangled a
piece of cheese over the mouse-
hole.

But Mrs Mouse hooked the
cheese into the hole with her
umbrella. She chuckled to
herself.

"What a cheeky mouse!"
said Clive.

Then he and Zot lay down
and snored.

Mrs Mouse thought they
were asleep. She came tripping
out of the mouse-hole, eating
the cheese.

She climbed on Zot's tail. She
was a very, very cheeky mouse.
Then she climbed on Zot's
back. Zot squinted at her from
one eye.

Mrs Mouse tiptoed on to
Zot's head! And then, quick as
a trick, Zot tossed her into the
air and caught her in his mouth.
Mrs Mouse squealed with
fright!

"You are a silly mouse,"
Clive said. "We might have
been cats and then we'd have
eaten you all up. But you *were*
clever with the cheese."

15

"I'll show you another trick,"
said Mrs Mouse.

"Another trick?"

"Yes," she said. "But first
you must put me down."

16

Zot gently put Mrs Mouse on the ground.

"Now close your eyes," she said.

When they opened them again, Mrs Mouse had disappeared! Zot woofed and said it was MAGIC. Clive just stared.

We know where that clever
mouse went, but we won't tell
Zot or Clive, will we?

Zot and
Old Duck

Down at the bottom of the lane, Zot met an old duck. Its feathers were dusty and droopy and its eyes were dull like old beads.

"I'm looking for Mrs Duck," it quacked huskily.

"What strange feet you have!" Zot said. "For a duck, that is."

"Didn't you know," said Old Duck, "that all old ducks grow paws?"

"No," Zot woofed. "And
what a strange mouth you
have, Old Duck. It's full of
teeth!"

"Didn't you know," said Old
Duck, "that all old ducks get
teeth?"

"No," Zot woofed. "And what a strange tail you have, Old Duck. It's furry at the tip!"

"Ah," replied the duck. "Didn't you know that all old ducks have furry-tipped tails?"

"No," said Zot. "Do they?"
He stared at Old Duck.

"Mrs Duck will recognize me
if you'll take me to her," Old
Duck said slyly. "One duck
always knows another, you'll
see."

So Zot led Old Duck round to
the pond, where Mrs Duck was
eating breakfast. As soon as
she saw Zot, she ruffled her
feathers and quacked –

"Who've you brought to see
me now?"

Old Duck tried to hide behind
Zot's back.

"It's one of your old friends,"
Zot said.

27

Mrs Duck waddled a little nearer.

"A duck with paws," Zot grinned.

Mrs Duck quickly waddled a few steps back.

"Paws?" she cried.

"Yes," Zot said. "Paws . . . and teeth."

"Hush!" hissed Old Duck.

Mrs Duck waddled away a
few more steps.

"Teeth?" she asked, in a
trembling voice. "You'll be
telling me next it's got a tail,
like Fowly Fox!"

"A tail . . ." Zot coughed.
"Well, as a matter of fact . . ."
"Grrr," growled Old Duck
crossly, lunging at Mrs Duck.

But Zot was standing on some of Old Duck's drooping feathers, and when Old Duck tugged, away they came . . . with lumps of red hair stuck to them, for under the feathers which he'd glued to his coat *was* Fowly Fox!

Mrs Duck let out a terrible squawk and clattered across the pond.

But Fowly Fox squawked
more! For his red coat was
peppered with bald spots.
And he'd lost his dinner!

"Woof!" Zot yapped crossly.
"Bah!" groaned Fowly Fox,
and slunk off into the wood.

"Quack quack," cried Mrs Duck from the safety of the pond. "It serves that old fox right."

"Well," said Zot happily. "I've heard of a wolf in sheep's clothing, but never a fox in duck's feathers!"

Zot and
Addy Snake

One day, Zot and Clive let
Madam Addy Snake come to
live in the shed at the bottom of
their garden.

"This is just right," she hissed. "Except for a door . . . It would be much warmer with a door that shut snugly and kept out the draughts."

"Woof," Zot said. "We'll make a new door for you if that would make you happy."

"Ssss . . ." said the snake
with a thin smile.

So Clive and Zot made a
good, strong door and fixed it
on the shed.

Zot and Clive felt happy as
they sat down to their tea. But
just then, Addy Snake came in
and whined, "Could I trouble
you to install a light in the shed,
so that I can see what I'm
doing?"

"Woof," said Zot. "You can borrow my lamp if you like." And he gave his lamp to the snake.

"Hiss," said Addy softly. "Thanksss, ZZZottt . . ." And she wriggled away to her new home.

No sooner had she gone, however, than back she came, hissing, "Have you any tea to spare, my friends, 'cos I haven't eaten for days and my tummy's rumbling and complaining?"

"Woof," Zot said. "Come and share our tea, Madam Snake."

So the snake wound her way up the table leg and, resting her head and half of her body on the table-cloth, she quickly swallowed all the food that remained. Flicking her forked tongue between her lips, she slid away, whispering, "G'night, friendsss."

Zot and Clive went to bed
hungry. But when they woke
up, Addy Snake was already in
the house, eating the last of
Zot's bones and Clive's cereal.

"Sssss," she said. "A lovely
morning; three of my friends
are coming today."

Zot barked crossly. He and
Clive had to go out and buy
some more food. On their way
back, they made a plan. When
they reached their little house,
there were *four* snakes lying on
the slabs by the front door . . .

"We's very hungry," they
hissed when they saw Zot's
meat and Clive's new loaf.
Clive winked at Zot. Zot
woofed at Clive.

"Have you ever tried Snake Pie, Zot?" Clive asked, behind his hand, but loudly enough for the snakes to hear. "If we give them my bread and your meat, think how much fatter they'll be!"

Zot wagged his tail.

Madam Addy began to turn a funny colour. "Ssss, did you hear that?" she muttered to her friends.

"Sssss," they replied. "Snake Pie!!"

"There's a nice strong door
on the shed," said Zot.

"And a light so they can't
hide in any dark corners," Clive
added in a loud whisper. "We
could trap them easily in
there."

"Would you and your friends like this food?" Clive asked the snakes.

"Sss, sss," they answered.

"Then follow us to the shed," he said. "It's much warmer there and you'll be more comfortable."

Zot and Clive ran ahead and
opened the door of the shed.
For a time they waited. But the
snakes did not come.

Zot grinned. "I think I'll go and see if they're coming!" he said and ran back to the house. But there was no sign of Madam Addy or her friends.

They had slithered away as
fast as they could!

"Snake Pie! Snake Pie!" they
hissed bitterly at Madam Addy.
"We're lucky to be alive!"

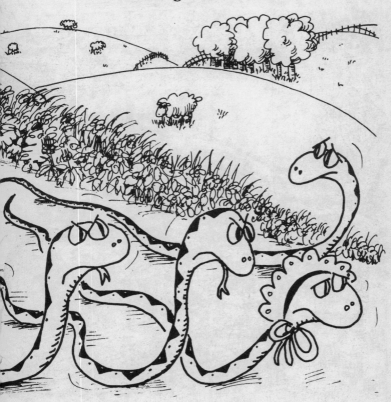

Clive locked the shed door.
He and Zot strolled slowly back
to their own small house and
ate a jolly good breakfast.

"Woof," said Zot. "Thank
goodness for that . . . I couldn't
bear to eat Snake Pie."

Could you?

Zot and Frog

One day, Zot ate a frog.
"You shouldn't do that," said
Clive. "It's germs!"
"I feel a bit funny," said Zot.

"Listen!"

CROAK! CROAK!

"Who said that?" asked Clive.

"I did," said Frog. "Let me out! It's dark in here and full of old bones."

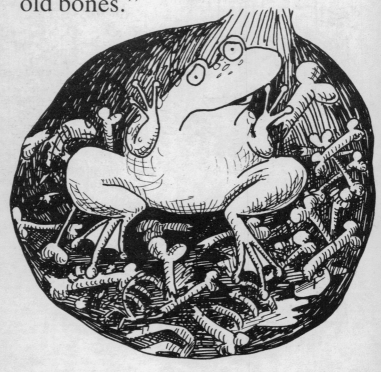

"You need a drink of water,"
Clive said to Zot, and fetched
the watering-can.

It didn't work.

"Let me out!" Frog yelled,
"or I'll swim about in your
tummy!"

"I think I need a frog-
escape," said Zot.

"Hang on," said Clive. "I've
got an idea – eat a duck and the
duck will eat the frog."

"Yeh, and who's going to eat the duck?" Frog croaked.

"Stand on your head, then," Clive said. "It might make him fall out."

Zot stood on his head.

"I don't like this," honked Frog. "Stop it! I'm upside-down!"

Zot lay on the grass.

"Ooh, I do feel dizzy!" he said.

"My missis will wonder where
I've got to!" Frog said. "She'll
be hoppin' mad, I can tell you!"

"Listen," said Clive, "I know
what!" He whispered
something in Zot's ear. Zot
opened his jaws wide so Clive
could shout down his throat . . .

"Hey Frog! There's a fly in
Zot's mouth!"
PIANGG!!

Frog jumped clean out of
Zot's tummy, flicking his
tongue.

"Told yer!" Clive shouted.
"Good one," agreed Zot.
Clive shook Zot's paw.
"Missed!" Frog croaked and
hopped crossly down the lane.

"Let's go home," said Clive.
"It's dinner-time."
"I couldn't eat a thing," Zot
whimpered.

When Frog got home, Mrs
Frog was waiting.
  "I was eaten. By a dog.
That's why I'm late," he said.
  But do you think Mrs Frog
believed him?!!

Zot and
Mrs Duck

In a little grassy hollow at the foot of a tree, Zot found an egg.

"Woof!" he said. "What's this?"

He nudged it with his nose. It rolled. Mrs Duck came scuttling.

"QUACK! QUACK! Get
away from my egg!"

"Your egg?" yapped Zot. "I
found it."

"I laid it!" snapped Mrs
Duck, and pecked Zot on the
nose.

"OW!" Zot yowled.

Mrs Duck sat on the egg.

"You'll break it!" warned Zot.

"Don't be silly!" said Mrs Duck. "Eggs like to be sat on."

Zot loped along to find Clive
hunting gold in the grass.

"Look!" called Clive. "I've
found an egg."

"Put it down!" squealed Zot.
"It's the duck's egg!"

"Put it down," Zot insisted,
"and let's sit on it."

"Sit on it?" asked Clive.

"Eggs *like* to be sat on," Zot
said.

"Don't be silly," said Clive,
but . . .

Zot sat on the egg!

"It feels very ODD. As if
something's sticking in me!"
said Zot.

Clive scratched his head. "I
told you not to sit on it."

"I think it must have
broken," Zot said.

"QUACK! QUACK!" Up
waddled Mrs Duck.

"Now we're for it," quivered
Zot.

Mrs Duck glared at Zot.
"Where's my egg?" she
demanded.

"OWCH!" Zot yelped and leaped into the air.

"That's what was pecking you!" Clive chuckled.

Mrs Duck started to titter.

"Hatched by yourself, did you?" she cooed.

"No, HE did it!" cheeped the duckling, pointing its tiny beak at Zot.

"Haven't you got your own eggs to sit on?" asked Mrs Duck as she waddled off for a swim in the pond.

"Bye-bye, Daddy," the duckling chirped, and wobbled after her.